The Grand Adventures of Sadie Mae Fuller Back Home

Brenda Wilder

DEDICATION

This book is dedicated to my grandchildren. Live the adventure.

CONTENTS

1

THE BIRTHRIGHT

"I will do it. I will teach the children." The voice yelled louder. " I said- I will teach the children." No one heard the voice from the back of the room because everyone was still talking loudly to fervently persuade other towns folk that their solution was the best. It was very difficult to make sense of what was being said. The mayor was in disbelief when he looked up and saw someone at the back of the room yelling to be heard. He raised his hands high in the air and said with a very loud voice, "Listen here everyone. I do believe someone here in the meetin' would like to speak."

Everyone turned around and saw her standing there with fear in her eyes, yet with a sense of determination. Some of the towns folk rolled their eyes when they realized who had been yelling from the back of the room. Others snickered but not enough to be heard much. The rest just shook their head in disapproval.

"Mayor Bradley, I will teach the children. I will be their teacher. You haven't found anyone yet and I happen to think that I would be best at learning these here fine youngin's. What better solution to the problem then to declare me the teacher of Smith…………"

The mayor quickly interrupted, "So what makes you think that you are qualified to teach these here children? I done knowed for a fact that you ain't qualified to be no teacher. Tell me that you are playin' some silly kind of notion in your head that just happened to come outta your mouth."

"Rest and assure yourself Mayor Bradley that I am not a crazy woman. We have ourselves a problem and I am just the right person to fix it. Now, you gonna let me teach these youngins or not? Mayor Bradley, though I might not have any formal schoolin', I feel that I'm the most qualified to teach these children because after all, this town is…..this town is…….."

"This town is what?"

" You know what, Mayor Bradley. Everyone in this town knows that it is named after my granddaddy – Jeremiah Rutherford Smith. And since I'm his kinfolk, I believe that it is my birthright to be this town's teacher."

"Myrtle, just because your granddaddy named this town after him doesn't qualify you to be no teacher. The matter is settled. We're gonna keep on lookin' till we find just the right person. Now go right on and sit yourself down. "

People started leaving the building as they were commenting on the absurdity of the situation. The mayor yelled to those leaving, "Please wait. We aren't finished with the meetin'. We'll have ourselves a solution soon. I'm almost certain we will." But it was too late. Everyone was already gone except the mayor and Myrtle.

"Mayor Bradley, I don't know why you're actin' like a stubborn old Missouri mule, but you are. I can do cipherin' in my head and I certainly know how to read-for the most part. I'd rather teach them what little I know than to have them learnin' nothin'. I reckon this should be none of my affairs, but I do care about the kids in this town and it certainly doesn't look good to the other towns around that we can't find a suitable teacher. Now you can continue to be stubborn, or just go right on ahead and let me teach. It's just that simple. It's only for a trial you know until we find ourselves a full-time teacher. At least while I'm the teacher, these kids could be learnin' something. Better learn something than nothin'. Don't you agree Mayor?"

"I'm sorry Myrtle, but the county school board would never allow anyone without them there teachin' qualifications to be the teacher. I know you mean well and have the utmost of best intentions, but I just can't allow you to do this. Nothin' against you Myrtle. It's just that you don't have a piece of paper saying you're qualified."

"Supposin' you are right mayor. I just don't think a piece of paper with my name scribbled on it by some high falutin' school says that I am or I ain't able to do anything. If you change your mind mayor, then you know where to find me."

The mayor stood there all alone in the building with no answers and no hope for a solution.

That morning for church, Amelia decided to stay in bed since she was a "little under the weather" following the trip to St. Louis. Frederick came back to the house and saw Amelia sitting on the couch still in her nightgown and robe sipping on a cup of hot tea.

"I see that you have finally got out of bed Miss Amelia. Perhaps if you'd like, we can take the car out for an afternoon drive. The weather is quite lovely for a particularly warm fall day."

"Why don't you go ahead without me Frederick. I just don't feel like going anywhere. I have something I would like to do today and I really would like to be alone, if you don't mind."

"If that's what you'd like, then I will leave after lunch."

"Perfect. So, how was church?"

"Church was fine indeed."

"Has the mayor found a replacement teacher?"

"No, Miss Amelia. He has not. However, a lady stood up and said that she would like to teach the children. She mentioned that she had the right to be the teacher because of some family of her founded this town. The mayor declared her unfit to teach and then everyone left the church building."

Amelia sat very still seemingly unaffected by the news she had just heard.

After lunch as Frederick was preparing for his afternoon drive,

Amelia said, "Frederick, what I need to do today will take some time so I would appreciate it if you would be gone for quite awhile. I know this seems like a very odd request, but please do know that I don't mean to hurt you. I just need to be alone to get this done."

"Yes ma'am," Frederick replied as he walked out of the house.

Amelia got up from the table and went to her bedroom and found the box of her wedding memories. Instead of delicately handling each memory with care, she made piles of them on her bed. She found her corsage of delicate white roses that she wore after her wedding. The brown, flat, shriveled, dried-out corsage had been carefully pressed and preserved. Amelia put it in the throw away pile. She saw her silver knife and cake server that she and Albert used to cut the cake and share a first piece as husband and wife. Amelia decided to put that in the share pile. She thought that someone could find a use for this fancy knife and server set. Next, she saw her wedding picture in its elegant wooden frame. She took the picture out of the frame and placed the frame with the other items going to the share pile. The picture that showed two people not really in love yet was placed on the throw away pile. On a happy day like a wedding, the bride and groom especially should look like they are happy, but the camera that caught this picture showed disappointment and loneliness. Amelia found the wedding picture book that had more pictures from the wedding and the grand reception at the Plaza Hotel. Everything about the wedding screamed status and business. Amelia always felt that her Aunt Jacqueline threw the most lavish wedding imaginable just to show off how much money she and uncle had obtained through lucrative banking deals. In the pictures, the wedding guests looked like they were enjoying the life of luxury at Amelia and Albert's expense.

Amelia went through each wedding item and designated it as share pile or throw away. Not once did she even shed a tear or reminisce about this day that caused her pain all over again. If anything at all, seeing these mementos made her angry all over again. Amelia saw the items that she collected from her honeymoon travel around the world. She was very tempted to put them all on the throw away pile, but she had a better idea for a couple of these little trinkets. She made another pile with a better purpose.

Brenda Wilder

2

AFTERNOON ADVENTURE

On the way home from church that morning, Elliot Sr. told Bev that he needed to stop at the auto repair shop to pick up a tool he needed to fix the tractor. The Fuller kids were sitting in the back of the old truck anxiously waiting to get home for some lunch.

Elliot Jr. said, "Guess this means we won't have to go to school tomorrow. I'm glad we get to stay home. Who needs school anyway?"

"Elliot, no one ever has to worry about wonderin' if you're silly. You just open your mouth, and there you go. Silly comes out every time," said Sadie.

"Well at least I'm not crazy like you are Sadie."

"You take that back. I'm not crazy."

"Kids, stop arguin' and fussin' with each other or else you can walk home."

"Thank you momma. They're annoying when they argue and all they do is argue. Can't you make them get along momma?", asked Mary.

"You kids put your hands over your mouth and don't say another word until we get home and then I'm not sure I wanna hear you talkin' then. My lands you children need to go back to school cause you're on my last nerve. I only have one nerve left and you kids are all over it."

When the Fuller family got back to their farm, the kids quickly jumped out of the truck and went their separate ways. Bev got right to work in the kitchen making lunch for the hungry family. She started to peel a pile of potatoes and thought about a great way to get this lunch fixed quicker. She yelled, "Sadie, Elliott, come on down here to the kitchen." No movement was heard. She yelled again and still no movement. Then she went to the living room and opened the rickety screen door. She stepped out onto the porch and yelled for them again.

"Sadie Mae and Elliot Jr. Fuller, you kids come here right now." This time they heard her and came from different directions. Sadie had been in the barn with her dad and Elliott was trying to make a sling shot out of a small twig that he found in the yard. It was the perfect shape for a sling shot and all he needed was something to help propel a rock or other object into the air.

As both Sadie and Elliott stood near the steps of the porch, Bev shared her brilliant idea with the kids. "Since you two are bent on pickin' on each other like chickens pickin' at rocks in the dirt, I have just the right thing to stop all this pickin'. Follow me please."

Elliott looked at Sadie with pure disgust because he knew what his mom meant by "just the right thing". That meant chores as punishment for his and Sadie's behavior. Sadie stuck her tongue out at Elliott to show her disapproval.

They followed Bev into the kitchen and she had them sit down at the table. She gave them each five potatoes, a paring knife, and exact instructions.

"Here you go kids. Peel these here potatoes and not one word to each other. You just sit there nice and quiet. Don't leave much potato on the skin. No wastin' now. I think a mess of fried potatoes sounds mighty delicious if I do say so myself. Hurry up now. We have some hungry mouths to feed".

Sadie and Elliot sat quietly while they peeled their five potatoes. They knew better than to say a word because mom meant business. Any breach in her direct orders would result in more chores.

After lunch was over, Sadie and Elliott had to clean off the table and wash the dishes. Elliott washed and Sadie dried. They didn't talk to each other the whole time because neither one of them wanted more chores to do.

Once the dishes were clean and put away, Sadie asked her momma, "Can I go to the creek? I wanna see if I can catch me a mess of fish or some crawdads."

"Yes Sadie, you can go. Make sure you are back in time for supper."

In no time, Sadie was out the door but not before stopping by the barn to pick up her cane pole, a net and then dig up a few worms to put in her worm bucket.

Sadie loved fishin' at the creek but she was particularly glad to have some quiet time to herself since getting back from St. Louis. She found her favorite spot where the fish bite every time. She put the worm

on the hook and plopped it down into the water. Sadie starred at the cork

floater bobbing up and down from the ripples made by the water. The

hypnotic movement of the floater in the water caused Sadie's mind to

think of other things rather than the fish nibbling at the worm on the

hook. Her mind was really not on fishin' at the moment, but rather she

started thinking about St. Louis.

She thought about the girls that had been digging through the

trash to find food, the little boy and his family waiting for their boat to

come, and how quiet was Miss Amelia was all the way back to

Smithfield. Sadie wondered if the girls would ever find a home again

and if someone would feed them. She thought about Miss Jim and the

wonderful things she saw at the zoo.

As she was deep in thought about the things she saw and heard

in St. Louis, she felt someone push her from behind, and yell, "boo".

She turned around really fast and saw Ernest standing there laughing at

what he had done. Sadie was so mad at him that she threw down her

pole, stood up, and punched him in the arm.

"Hey, now what did ya go and do that for? You didn't have to hit

me. I just startled ya."

"You scared me to death Ernest. Don't ever do that again. You're such a weirdo Ernest. What kind of person goes around startlin' people?"

"This kind Sadie. Watch this."

Ernest hopped up onto a log near the edge of the water and was acting like he was walking the tight rope seen at one of those circus shows. He held out his arms to help balance himself on the log. He was somewhat steady on the log walking forward and back. Ernest looked at Sadie as he was showing off and said, "See Sadie, lookie here. I can walk on this here log and no net to catch me if I fall."

"Don't be silly Ernest. It's not that high off the ground. If you did fall………."

And right at that very moment, Ernest's foot slipped out from under him and he waved his arms furiously to keep his balance, but it was too late. He hit the ground pretty hard. Ernest's body lay there on the rocky ground and he was as still as a door stop.

Sadie ran over to him screaming his name, "Ernest, Ernest, are you alright?" She put her hand on his chest to feel if he was breathing. She didn't feel any movement at all or it could have been that she was so scared she didn't know if she could feel him breathing or not. Sadie started to cry because she thought that Ernest was dead from this senseless act of showing off just for her. Sadie laid her head on Ernest's chest as she sobbed uncontrollably. She raised her head quickly when she heard a deep moaning sound. Ernest's eyes were slightly moving and he started blinking.

"Oh Ernest. Ernest, can you hear me. Are you dead? Don't die Ernest. I'd feel so bad that I hit you. Ernest, wake up."

Ernest blinked a couple of more times and then let out another deep groan. He finally opened his eyes enough to see Sadie leaning over him with tears in her eyes. Ernest knew that this was his one chance, his one and only opportunity to do what he's been wanting to do for a long time. His courage was enough this time to propel him to do the unthinkable. He raised his head high enough to plant a kiss on Sadie's cheek.

Sadie just sat still for a second and then said, "Why Ernest if you weren't almost dead from fallin', I'd knock you out. Why did you go and do that for?"

"It just felt like the thing to do. Besides, I've wanted to do that my whole life. Sadie Mae Fuller I like you. You're just the bees knees.

Why Sadie, I've liked you for a long time and...."

"I have bee knees? What kind of sayin' is that. Don't ever kiss me again or else I'll tell my daddy on you and he'll have a talkin' to your dad. Ernest you make me so, so, so....."

"So what Sadie. I make you so what. Go ahead and say it, but I know that you can't because you like me too."

"I don't like you Ernest. That's the silliest thing I done ever heard. Now stop talkin' all crazy. You must have bumped your head real good."

"Nope. I didn't bump my head at all. I like you and you like me and we both knowed it. Now just accept the fact that we like each other and someday......someday......someday."

"Someday what Ernest?"

"Aw, nothin'. It's nothin'. Guess I reckon I should be gettin' back home since it's gettin' closer to supper time and my folks will be wonderin' where I am." Ernest started to walk away but he seemed sad. He wondered if he had missed an opportunity that might never come this way again, or would it perhaps.

As Ernest was walking away, Sadie yelled, "Do you want me to walk with you just to be sure you're ok or somethin'?"

"Na, I'm fine. You go on and keep fishin'. His voice was trailing off the further he got away from Sadie. With his head still hung low, he said in a quiet voice, "I will marry you someday Sadie Fuller. If only I had the courage to ask. But will you Sadie have the courage to say yes."

3

FORGET ME – FORGET ME NOT

Amelia went through all of her wedding mementos and made appropriate piles according to her liking. She had a pile of things to take to the share pile, a pile of things with a special purpose, and another pile of things to throw away. As Amelia was putting items into bags and boxes, she had an idea that might help put some of her feelings and thoughts into perspective. She finished putting the items away and then took out a piece of paper to write a note to Frederick.

Dearest Frederick,

I am gone to see Ida Foster for awhile. I have questions and she has answers. Please do me a favor and take these boxes and bags and do accordingly. The bags on the kitchen table need to be taken outside and burned. Do not look in the bags. Do not take anything out of the bags. Throw these bags on a burn pile and do not retrieve anything out of those bags. The boxes by the door need to be taken to the share pile. Likewise with the bags, do not go through these boxes. Put the boxes on the share pile and walk away. These are all my items to do with as I please and this is what I intend to do. The smaller box can be put in the closet on the top shelf. I will work with it later on. I will see you when I return from Ida's. I will probably have supper there since she will insist, I'm sure.

Frederick, you are a dear friend and I trust that you will carry out my wishes with no questions asked.

Sincerely yours, Amelia

Amelia put the note on the kitchen table, locked the door, and walked to Ida's house. As Amelia was walking, she felt as if she has the weight of the world lifted off of her shoulders. She thought at first that she should have been guilty for what she had done, but she didn't at all. This was in fact the first time that Amelia felt like she had control over her own life and no one was going to lie to her ever again. Amelia finally arrived at Ida's house – a place she hadn't seen for awhile. She knocked on the familiar door and waited. The door opened and she was greeted by someone she knew who would be honest with her.

"Well my lands child. I haven't seen you in what seems like a coons age. I told you when you moved away with that butler of yours to make sure you stop by for a spell and see me. I am sure glad to see you though for it has been awhile."

"I know Ida. I'm so very sorry that I've not stopped by, but I am here now."

"Come on in and sit. Let me take a look at you. My, oh my you sure look nice today. Missed seeing you at church this morning. I'll tell you all about that later. Please tell me all about St. Louis. Did you have a nice time? Did Sadie like St. Louis? Did you see your uncle? Oh lands, I am asking a lot of questions. There's no one been in the boarding house for weeks and I done feel like I talk to the walls just to hear some noise."

"That's ok Ida. I don't mind answering your questions as long as you don't mind answering a few of mine. To start with, St. Louis was fine. Sadie did have a good time. She saw much more of life outside of Smithfield than she expected - some of it good, and some of it not so good. I sure wish I could shelter her from this old world but I know I can't. I hope Sadie sees things for what they really are, when she gets older of course. I did see Edward and that is partially why I am here. He told me the truth about everything he did and how he was partly responsible for Albert's death. He lied to me too and paid me off as a way to ease his guilt. I will not help him ease his conscience any more.

I won't take another dime from that dishonest man. Of all Albert's family, he treated me like I was a real part of the family. The others hated me because of what Aunt Jacqueline did to them.

Ida, let's get to the real reason why I'm here because I need answers. First of all, what happened to my parent's belongings? I'm sure they had things in that house, but I need to know what happened to them. Ida, please don't keep anything from me. I've been lied to long enough and I'm in the right frame of mind right now to hear the truth. Trust me, it can't get any worse than what I heard from Edward."

Ida paused for a few moments. She hung her head down for she knew that this day would come eventually. She began, "Well, when your momma and daddy got sick with the pleurisy, they made arrangements with your aunt to come and get you and give you a proper upbringing in New York. This you all know, but I'm just drawing a line of events here for you to follow. Then one day your Aunt Jacqueline came to pick you up. Helen had not gone to the grave yet, but she was certainly close considering how bad she and your daddy were. Your aunt stayed here at the house until they passed, God rest their souls. As soon as they were gone, she took you off to New York. You left with nothing but the clothes you had on. I'm not so sure that she didn't change your clothes as soon as she got you got away from Smithfield. She was certainly in a hurry to leave."

"Ida, what about their things? What did she do with their things?"

"I'm getting to that part. Don't rush me child. Your aunt wasn't too far down the road. Couldn't have been more than a stone's throw away and then two men showed up at your momma and daddy's house. They took everything out of the house to the back yard. They made a big pile out of all of it and set it to fire. Everything out of that house was burned down to ashes. She tried to give your momma and daddy's things away to most of the towns folk, but we all thought it was not right. Not right at all. And since we wouldn't take anything, she burned it. Your aunt said that she wanted no part or memory of this town with the exception of you. Your presence around her was not much of a Smithfield memory because she worked hard to change you into a picture of refinement. What she did was wrong, but it's what she thought she had to do. I'm sorry to tell you what must be most painful and heart breaking, but my dear one, it is the truth. You deserve to know what really happened."

Amelia just sat there starring out into the distance trying to process in her head what she had just heard. Amelia had no idea how her aunt could live in good conscience from her horrible actions. "Ida, I appreciate your honesty. You are the only person besides Frederick who I can trust. My life of lies has led me to a path of nothing. And the crazy thing is that I didn't choose this path. It was chosen for me. This path of lies was forced upon me just so others could seek their own fortune and hide from their own guilt. Now what, Ida? Now what do I do with this life that has not one ounce of truth to it? I refuse to take any more money from Edward because he is paying off his guilt. Well, no thank you. I'm done, but I don't know where to go now."

"Amelia my dear one, I wish I could take this pain away from you and make it all better, but I can't. I just can't. But one thing I can do for you is to help you get back on your feet to a path of truth and honesty. I'm sure there is something out there for a woman such as yourself. Well, I'm almost certain there is. I just need to think a little and then it will come to me. Ida, use your brain that God gave you and think of something."

Ida piddled around the kitchen in deep thought as she was trying to think of the exact thing that could help Amelia start a new life full of truth – no lies any more.

"You will join me for supper won't you Miss Amelia? I'll not take no for an answer. Not been much company here at the boarding house for weeks. An old lady can't eat alone every night until she starts talking to anything that will stand still long enough to listen. Everything in this house is standing still, so I just talk to it like it's been a long lost friend."

"Sure, Ida. I will stay for supper. I appreciate the invitation most gracefully."

"I'm glad then. How 'bout you help me cut up these here vegetables?"

Ida handed a pile of turnips, carrots, celery, and a paring knife. Amelia began to peel, cut, and chop away at the vegetables. Both of them sat very still in deep thought while preparing food for supper. Amelia concentrated intently on every movement of her hand as the knife cut through the vegetables. All was oddly quiet for Ida's house, but she too was concentrating on searing the meat in a cast iron skillet before putting it in the oven to finish cooking.

All of a sudden Ida yelled out with excitement, "I've got it. I know exactly what it is. Why didn't I think of this much sooner. Why Ida old gal, you sure have nailed this one right on the head. It's a pure stroke of genius thought going on in this here head of mine right now. Amelia, I know exactly what you can do. I can't believe it's been here all along right underneath our own noses. My lands, if it were a snake, I'd a done been bit. This is the solution to many a problem in this old town and in that broken-to-pieces heart of yours. Yes, indeed. I have the answer."

Ida told Amelia her idea and they both began to plan what to do next. Indeed it was a solution to many a problem in Smithfield – at least it was to Ida and Amelia.

4

THE CLEANSING CHANGE

Sadie ran most of the way back home because she had something very important to do and it couldn't wait a second longer. She was exhausted from running the whole way, but her need was urgent- so she felt. Once she reached her house, clearly out of breath, she flew open the screen door and ran straight for the medicine cabinet. Sadie grabbed a bottle and then ran back outside. She went behind the house, found a small tin cup, and then filled it with water from the rain barrel. She stood at the barrel and emptied some of the bottle's content into her hand and began to rub it fiercely on her cheek. She put a little more of the oil in her hands and rubbed her cheek again until it was almost raw. Then she took some of the water and rubbed it into her cheek as well.

As Sadie was concentrating on scrubbing her cheek, she didn't notice that Mary had been watching her for a little while-at least long enough to notice Sadie's odd behavior.

"What on earth are you doin' Sadie?"

Sadie jumped from being startled and scared to death. She looked up to see Mary standing nearby with a strange look on her face.

"Uh…..nothin'. What makes you think I'm doin' anything?"

"You've been standing there scrubbin' your face like an old dog scratching at ticks. What's goin' on and what do you have in your hand?"

"It's nothin'. Leave me alone. Go back in the house right now. I mean it."

"I ain't doin' no such thing. You're up to somethin' and you're gonna tell me what it is. If you don't then I'm gonna go tell momma."

"No! Don't tell her. Don't tell anyone. I just got somethin' on my face and I just need to wash it off."

Mary reached down and grabbed the bottle out of Sadie's hand. "Castor oil? What in the world are you doin' puttin' castor oil on your face?"

"I can't tell. I just need to get somethin' off my face that's all. Now go back in the house."

"Sadie Fuller, what did you do to your face?"

"I didn't do nothin'. Honest Abe I didn't."

"Then why in the world are you scrubbin' your face and why do you have this bottle of castor oil? Come on, tell me or else I'll go get momma."

"Mary, you are just mean. Just plain mean." Sadie began to cry. "I don't wanna tell you 'cause you're just gonna go tell everyone."

Mary finally knew that this was serious because Sadie didn't cry much unless it's was something that really upset her. So she went over to Sadie and put her arm around her. "Let's set here Sadie and tell me what has you so bugged."

Sadie looked up at Mary with astonishment. "I was fishin' down at the creek. I was thinkin' about St. Louis and them two hungry girls. I was thinkin' about the little boy and his family waitin' for their boat. My mind wasn't much on the fish. Ernest snuck up on me and scared me half to death. He was showin' off on the old log. He was pretendin' like he was walkin' on the high wire like those circus folk do. His foot slipped out from underneath him and down he went. I thought he was dead. He didn't move but then all of a sudden, he woke up and kissed me on the cheek. That rascal. And now I've been defiled with cooties. I'm tryin' to wash off them cooties with castor oil. Now you'll have to walk in front of me and yell, unclean, unclean."

"What do you mean by that Sadie?"

"You know like that story in the Bible that I heard the preacher talk about. He said that in the Bible days, people would walk in front of the leopards and yell unclean cause them leopards were sick. Well, I guess you can walk in front of me from now on and yell unclean because I'm definitely down with the cooties. See, look at my cheek. It's all spotted red and now I'm a sick leopard. I'm not sure it's workin'. Maybe I need to do more scrubbin'. Now you're gonna go tell everyone that Ernest kissed me aren't you."

Mary looked at Sadie and gently said, "No, Sadie. I won't tell a soul. I pinky swear I won't. Here, let me help you scrub." Mary took her apron and wiped off the oil and water that was left on Sadie's face.

5

A BRAND NEW LIFE

The next morning, Amelia woke up and asked Frederick to fix breakfast for her earlier than normal. She told Frederick that she had some business to tend to and needed to leave in a hurry. She quickly ate her breakfast and rushed out the door. Amelia found herself once again calling on the mayor of Smithfield without an appointment.

"Good morning Sally Jean. Is the mayor in this morning? Can I speak to him please? I know I do not have an appointment, but I don't think he's going to mind not one bit."

"Good mornin' to you Miss Amelia. I'm sure the mayor is here somewheres. At least he was here. I'll go fetch him for ya. If you just sit and wait right here, I'll be right back."

"Thank you Sally Jean."

A few minutes later Sally Jean came back to the office followed close behind by the mayor.

"Well howdy do Miss Amelia. What brings you to my office on this fine day?"

"Mayor Bradley, can we talk in your office please? I have something urgent to discuss with you."

"Why certainly we can. Sally Jean, hold all my appointments until later. I'm sure it's not going to be too busy around here. Folks are busy thinkin' about how to solve our little problem so I reckon it's keepin' their minds busy. It seems that Miss Amelia here has some urgent business and it seems like it can't wait a minute longer."

"Yes, mayor. I'll hold your appointments just fine cause you have none."

The mayor invited Amelia to his office and he shut the door behind them. He knew as did Amelia that this conversation would be anything but private with Sally Jean nearby. Amelia began the conversation.

"Mayor Bradley, it has come to my attention that you have not found a suitable replacement for Miss Boxx. I am submitting my interest in this position to you. I would like to teach the children of Smithfield. I am highly qualified to teach and I would love the opportunity to contribute to the proper education of these students. I have spent years at the university studying world cultures and I have also traveled the world in search of a broader understanding of what and who makes up the world. This should be an immediate decision since you have found no one. The answer couldn't be any easier than just saying a simple yes. I have so much to offer the students. I could expand their horizons with the knowledge I have gained from my worldly travels. Did I mention that I have traveled the world? I've seen oh so many wonderful things and have met so many interesting people. Oh Mayor Bradley, please say yes. I would be eternally and most definitely grateful for this opportunity."

The mayor sat for a minute before he offered his response to Amelia's plea.

"I don't think it's that bad of an idea. It's kinda growin' on me. And, I haven't found anyone yet with your credentials. Who knows, these youngins need a little sophistication and proper education from someone such as yourself. However, you do know that the towns folk will have to make a vote. Winnin' their approval won't be no easy task.

"I know Mayor Bradley, but I think I am up to the challenge of winning their approval. I'm not sure why I haven't thought of this before, but I think it's because I had no reason to be useful and now and do. Besides, I can use the……….. Exactly how much does it pay mayor?"

"Them details can be ironed out later, but I'm sure you're not worried about the money. I'm gonna call a town meetin' and we will have ourselves a vote. I don't know what the outcome will be, but I'll be pullin' for ya. I think you'd be a mighty fine teacher for these here kids."

"Thank you mayor. I appreciate your kind words of approval."

The mayor personally drove to each home of the town board members to announce that he's calling a town meeting tomorrow night at 6:00 pm. He knew that he had to have a very convincing argument for hiring Amelia. He knew that she was the only suitable option, but he also knew that the towns folk distrusted outsiders. And to them, Amelia was still an outsider.

All of the town board members showed up in time for the meeting at the school house. They were all talking at the same time wondering what this meeting is all about. No one knew because the mayor didn't tell them. Mayor Bradley arrived precisely at 6:00 pm on the dot. He walked to the front of the room and raised his hands to quiet the men.

"I'm supposin' you are all wonderin' why you've been called to this special meetin'. Well, let's just get right down to why we're here. I believe we have ourselves a teacher. She's been under our noses right here the whole time, but no one thought to look. Miss Amelia Cummings came to my office yesterday and expressed her deepest interest in becoming our teacher. She has the credentials to be a teacher and has the experience to go with it. I move that we hire Miss Amelia Cummings to be our teacher. All in favor, say aye."

Deep down the mayor knew this wasn't going to be easy, and he was right.

Ernie Jenkins stood up and said, "Mayor Bradley this isn't that easy. How do we know she's tellin' you the truth. Maybe it's some concocted story she's come up with to fool you into hirin' her. What kind of credentialin' does she have?"

The other men began to ask the mayor questions out loud. No one could be heard because they were all talking at the same time. The

mayor raised his hands again. The talking continued and no one was

paying attention to the mayor. He finally slammed his fist on the desk

and yelled, "Let this meetin' come to order. Men, we have got to listen

and talk instead of yellin'. Now, does anyone have anything to say in

favor of hiring Miss Amelia?"

The men all looked around at each other wondering who would

have the right mind to say something positive about Amelia. Elliot stood

up and began. "I will Mr. Mayor. I have some words to say. Miss

Amelia is a fine woman who has the proper up bringin' to be a teacher.

She's traveled all over the world and I one do believe that she is the

solution to our problem. My Sadie had written a paper about what she

did over the summer and Miss Boxx absolutely hated the paper. I know

that Sadie can be a handful, especially when she sets her mind to

somethin', but the paper wasn't graded on Sadie's spellin' and writin'.

No sir. It was graded on the fact that Sadie wants to see the world like

Miss Amelia has. I went to talk to Miss Boxx and she would not budge.

Not even a smidgen on the grade she put on that paper. I was gonna go

back to that school and finish my words with her, but she had gone done

and broke that leg. She told me that our kids are plain ignorant and their

papers were horrible. She's no fit for teachin' but I know that Miss

Amelia…..well, she'll do a mighty fine job. After all, she is one of our very own. You folks seem to forget that she's from this town too. She has every right to be here as each one of us do. Now, I think we should give her a try. If anything doesn't suit well, then I think we can reconsider and in the meantime Mr. Mayor, you can keep looking in case you know, it doesn't work out.

The room became even louder after Elliott spoke. The mayor had to quiet the room down once again. "Now listen here men, let's take a vote to see if we will even give Miss Amelia the chance to teach. Maybe on a trial basis like Elliott said. We can re-evaluate her capacity to teach and then meet again to decide a final outcome. All in favor say aye. Now I do believe we have made ourselves a decision in all agreement." No one had the chance to say aye or nay because the mayor didn't give them the opportunity to do so. "I will tell Miss Amelia myself tomorrow. She will be happy as a clam that is not in the stew pot. Men, you are dismissed."

The men were stunned by the mayor's ability to do a lot of fast talking and leaving them no time to speak. Once that mayor sets his mind to something, there's no moving him.

The very next day, the mayor went to Amelia's house. He arrived a little after breakfast, before Frederick could get everything cleared off the dining room table. The mayor knocked on the door and Frederick let him in. "My dear man, how are you on this fine mornin'. Is Miss Amelia here? I'd like to have a word with her. She's not expectin' me, but that's ok. I have some news to bring."

"Yes Mr. Mayor, she is here. I believe she is in her room. I'll let her know you are here." Frederick found Amelia exactly where he thought she would be and announced the mayor's presence. Amelia flew off of her chair and ran into the parlor where the mayor was waiting. Just before she got to the parlor, she straightened her dress and fluffed the ends of her hair. She saw the major standing by the fireplace looking at some pictures on the mantle.

"Hello mayor. How are you on this fine day?"

"I'm just fine Miss Amelia. I have some news to share with you and I just couldn't wait one more minute. We had ourselves a vote and we've decided that you can teach the children, but on a trial basis. After the trial, then we shall decide if we want to have you be their full-time teacher. It's just a formality to keep the naysayers from ruining everythin'. But I do have my ways of over ridin' their negativity. I've actually honed it into a skill I'm quite proud of. Now, let's sit down here and discuss the details of our agreement. Now with this here being a Wednesday and all, we should start school on Monday. That will give you enough time to at least come up with a lesson or two and enough time for the kids to enjoy a couple more days off. They've been off long enough, but a couple more days won't hurt, now will it. You just go on and start plannin' what you're going to teach. Let me warn you though, you would have had some nays if I would have let them speak, but you know how these things can get. I'm sure you'll do a fine job and we won't have to worry about no vote later on. It's a perfect matchin' that I should have thought about a lot sooner. Oh well. At least we have you now. I will find me some folks to help spread the news that school is about to start again. I'm most obliged to you Miss Amelia for stepping up in this time of crises."

6

WHAT JUST HAPPENED?

Amelia stood there stunned at the news she just heard. She was hoping

beyond all hopes that she would be selected to be Smithfield's newest

teacher, but actually hearing the words, "you're hired" took on a whole

new meaning for Amelia. She would have her first real job making her

very own money. Up until this time, someone else supported Amelia so

she relied on others to take care of her. Now, she can take care of

herself. Amelia was elated at the thought of being financially

independent for the first time in her life.

After the fogginess cleared from her thoughts, her mind began to race with ideas for her first day of class. She walked around the house as if she had never been in that house before looking for just a piece of paper and something to write with. She finally found the paper and a pencil that needed to be sharpened. She picked up the pencil and starred at the very dull charcoal. Amelia yelled with an urgency in her voice for Frederick. He came in a hurry thinking something was horribly wrong. He saw Amelia standing there holding the pencil and her hand was shaking.

"What is the matter Miss Amelia? Why are you shaking? Do I need to go get the doctor?"

"No Frederick. I just spoke with the mayor and he told me that I'm hired. I'm the new teacher. I just can't believe they hired me. Can you sharpen my pencil?"

Frederick gently removed the pencil from Amelia's shaking delicate hand. He held her hand for a moment and then gave her a hug. He sweetly said, "I'm very proud of you. Not just for this, but you have had many disappointments in this life and you seem to rise above each and every time. You Miss Amelia are a survivor."

Amelia quickly pushed Frederick away. "I have a thousand things to do. I'm not sure where to start. Maybe I could introduce myself. No, they know who I am. Perhaps I could teach them to speak French.

Suppose the class could write a paper about the president. Maybe they

could all dress in uniform. I could have them give speeches and write

dissertations about the economy. Maybe I could……..”

Frederick gently yet firmly held Amelia by the shoulders. “Miss

Amelia, I know your mind is racing with excitement, but do not forget,

this is Smithfield. These young minds have not had the privileges that

you have had. I'm not so sure that the town board agreed to your

appointment 100%. Why I'm almost certain that the mayor strong-

armed the board into letting you teach. You should walk lightly on this

delicate soil until they've made a solid decision.”

“Frederick, are you telling me that I'm not qualified? Do you doubt

my ability to teach these children some of the finer things in life? Just

whose side are you on Frederick? I simply cannot believe what I'm

hearing. Of all people, I thought that I would have your support. It is

clear and evident that I do not.”

“Miss Amelia, I didn't mean it that way. I'm just telling you to be

careful that's all. These people are hard working folk who aren't used to

anything fancy or a fancy new way of learning. Take your time to win

their loyalty. Do that by learning who they are. I mean really learning.”

"You just leave the teaching to me. You stick to driving and making sure that this place is kept in order. Now if you would leave me so that I may work on the first day's lesson. Perhaps Frederick you could think about where your loyalty lies."

Frederick slowly walked out of the room and out the front door. He went for a walk to clear his mind. He knew that Amelia was going in the wrong direction and his feeble attempt at steering her the right way was disastrous.

Amelia finished writing her lesson plan for the first day. It had been a while since she studied teaching at the university. Her lesson plan skills were a little rusty. She had eraser marks all over the paper.

Her very first lesson looked like this:

Introduce myself.

Teach them how to say good morning in French.

Teach them to count in French.

Have them introduce themselves.

Cover the rules for the classroom.

Have the students write the rules in perfect penmanship.

Plan speech topics.

Recite times tables through ten.

Spelling list.

Lunch.

American Government and Citizenship.

Review classroom rules.

Dismiss.

Amelia's lesson plan was perfect on paper, but was it going to be perfect for the children of Smithfield.

Amelia worked very hard on her lesson plan. She made notes on her notes and more notes on top of that. She felt nervous and excited all at the same time. It kinda felt like bees and butterflies whirling around in her stomach.

The mayor had made almost all his rounds to the families in Smithfield who had children. His last couple of stops was near the Fuller farm. Mayor Bradley drove up the dirt road and came to a stop right near Elliot's truck. He got out of his car and walked to the front porch. He tapped on the old wooden screen door a few times. Bev came to the door wiping her hands on her apron.

"Why Mayor Bradley, what brings you out to our humble home on this here fine day?"

"Is Elliot home? I need to have a word with him and the children if they are indeed here. Are they all here by chance? It is mighty important that I share a bit of news with the children and while I'm here, I might as well have a word or two with your husband."

"Fine, Mayor Bradley. I will go fetch them as they are all here indeed. Let me pour you a glass of water before I round them up. I'm sure you are athirst after that long ride out here. I will be right back with your water and members of the family."

The mayor waited a few minutes for his glass of water. After he sipped a little on the water, one by one the Fuller family came inside the house and sat near the mayor. They greeted him with a little trepidation not knowing why he was here calling on the Fuller family. Elliot came into the living room wiping his greasy, oily hands on an old dish rag that had seen better days.

"Mr. Mayor I am glad that you have made the journey out here today. I reckon I know why you've come a callin'. Has to do with that new………."

"Uhhum, uhhum, uhhum. Yes, it does. I intend to make a formal announcement once everyone is in here. Don't suppose you know when that will be do ya? I do have other places to visit before nightfall."

Sadie was the last of the Fuller family to arrive for the meeting. She stood in the living room behind the mayor while the others sat either on the couch or in a spare rocking chair. The mayor raised his hands to quiet the noise from the family talking.

"Well now I suppose you are all wonderin' why I came all the way out here on this fine day. Let's just get right to the point. We had ourselves a town meetin' yesterday and we have all decided and agreed upon that Miss Amelia should on a temporary basis be our new school teacher."

Thud.

" We will see how she does and how things go for a three month trial. After that time, we will decide if she is fit to be teachin'. If so, then she will continue teachin'. If we find her unfit, then we will have to look for someone else to teach. So, with that in mind dear children, you will be going back to school on Monday. You had yourselves a nice little extra vacation, but now it's back to learnin'. I'm sure you are more excited than you can hardly stand. How about you Sadie? Are you excited? Sadie? Sadie? Where did that child go?

7

LIFE LESSONS

"Sadie, where are you? My goodness that child was just standin' here listenin' to my big news and now she done gone."

Elliot Sr. said, "Mayor, she's on the floor. Look down and you'll see her."

The mayor looked down and saw Sadie's limp, lifeless body lying on the floor. He let out a squeal of shock and surprise. Then got down real close to her to see if she was breathing or not. He didn't see any movement at all. "Lookie there, Miss Sadie done give up the ghost. My condolences to you and yours. Was she sick or somethin'?"

"No mayor", replied Elliot Sr. "She is not sick or dead. She's just fine. Whenever Sadie gets excited, she faints. The news of Miss Amelia being her teacher was probably more than her little soul could handle. She'll be alright. Just give her a minute or two and she'll snap right on out of this here faintin' spell. We've come quite used to it by now. She done it for as long as we can remember."

Elliot Jr. piped up, "She's just fakin' it. She does that for attention. And look, she got just what she wanted – attention. If you'd stop makin' such a fuss over her faintin' spells, then she wouldn't do them no more. But there you go as usual – makin' a big fuss over what. Over nothin' I tell ya."

"Elliot Jr., you go on and hush you mouth", said Bev. "She is not fakin'. Doc says that she gets so excited that she just falls down. Sometimes we have to tell her important stuff while she's sittin' down. Less faintin' that way you know."

Still, the mayor couldn't continue with the details of his new found school teacher until Sadie returned to her normal self. He just kept watching for her chest to move up and down with breaths. He still wasn't convinced that she hadn't given up the ghost. He then saw something that caught his attention. He thought he had seen an eye twitch. He looked closer and asked the others if they had seen it. Once again Sadie's eye did twitch. Then she slowly opened her eye oh so very little. The mayor let out another yell. "Lookie there. She ain't dead after all. She is alive."

Sadie blinked a few more times and then looked around. She had a confused look on her face that seemed to convey that she had no idea where she was at or what had happened. "Why am I on the floor?", she asked. "Oh, I must have had one of them spells again. Mr. Mayor, what are you doin' here? Is somethin' wrong?"

"No Sadie. Everything is alright. Alright indeed. I just came callin' on you and your folks with some pretty excitin' news. Why don't you just stay on that floor right here and I'll tell you my big news. You see, Miss Amelia is going to be your new school teacher. Yes, indeed she is. She starts Monday. You kids will be back in school on Monday. You've had a nice long extrie break. It's bout time you all get yourselves on back at that school house. I think she'll do a fine job, but there are some you know who don't think so as much. So, we will try a temporary arrangement to see if she can do the job. But we are not gonna worry ourselves about that for now. No siree. We are just gonna get you kids back in school and everything is goin' to work out just fine."

"Oh, Mayor Bradley", said Sadie. That's the best news I ever done heard. Maybe I'm dreamin' or somethin'. Oh, please say it again. Say it again Mr. Mayor."

"Yes my dear one, you heard me correct. Miss Amelia is going to be your teacher for a few months that is until we can come to an agreement that she is just right for this job. But in the meantime, get rested up for school is gonna start Monday. Well, you fine folks have a nice day. I have a couple more things to do before suppertime. Elliot, if you have any questions or notice anything out of sorts, you let me know, but I am rest assured that she will do a fine job. Well, good night everyone."

Sadie ran to her room, slammed the door, and flung herself onto her bed. She reached under her pillow for her writing journal. She opened to a fresh new page and began to write.

Dear God,

I am the happiest of all your creatures today. You see, the mayor done come by today and told us all that Miss Amelia is going to be our new school teacher. No more mean Miss Boxx. Not sure she could teach anyway with her leg all done broke up. I can hardly stand the excitement. I can't wait for school to start on Monday.

Love, Sadie

Most excited person in the whole wide world

Sadie put her writing journal back underneath her pillow and the soft gentle feel of the pillow beckoned her to rest her head there for a short nap. Sadie dreamed of how grand and glorious school would be from now on with Miss Amelia at the helm.

Sadie was suddenly awakened from her sweet dreams by the sound of her momma yelling that supper was ready. Momma had fixed a big old pot of thick rabbit stew. She had made some biscuits to go with the stew and some freshly churned butter. Everyone ate a hearty helping of stew. There was hardly any talking during supper because they all were enjoying their meal.

Sadie was the first to break the silence. "I am so excited about Miss Amelia being our school teacher. I dreamt of how much fun school is gonna be from now on. No more mean teachers for us. No sir."

Elliot Jr. piped up, "Shut up Sadie. She's not gonna be a good teacher. What does she know about teachin' anyway? Not much I guarantee that."

"Elliot Jr., don't talk to your sister that way", said Elliot Sr.. You don't know yet how Miss Amelia teaches. You might learn somethin' after all rather than cause mischief. Just give her a chance you just might be pleasantly surprised."

Bev interrupted, "Just what does that mean? Sounds like Miss Amelia has your head turned as well. That's about right for that young woman. She'll do anything to……."

"Enough Bev! This is not the time or place to let your green with envy jealous feathers rare up and cause a stir where there is no stirrin' necessary."

Bev stomped to the kitchen with an arm full of dishes from the table to be washed, dried, and put away. You could hear her grumble ever so slightly from the living room. By the sound of the grumbling, she wasn't happy.

Monday morning finally came. Bev didn't have to wake up Sadie. She was already awake, dressed, and ready to go. The rest of the kids were harder to wake up since they were used to sleeping in until 7:00. Bev fixed a full breakfast of eggs and oatmeal. Sadie was too excited to eat much. Bev insisted that she eat more than enough to feed a small sparrow. She knew that by 9:00 Sadie would be hungry again if she didn't eat well. Elliot Sr. took the kids into town in his old rickety truck. Once they arrived at the school house, Sadie jumped out before the truck came to a complete stop. She ran to the school house and waited not so patiently at the door until Miss Amelia would come out to ring the bell. Sadie waited for what seemed like hours for that old oak door to creek open.

At last she saw the door knob turn. The door slowly opened and there stood Miss Amelia looking like a royal queen in her Sunday finest. She looked down and saw only Sadie standing at the foot of the steps waiting to go through the "golden gate" leading to a fine and worthy education. Amelia's eyes glanced down and she gave Sadie a subtle wink. Not a wink to be overly noticed by others who might have happened to look their way. Amelia tugged gently on the rope tied to the large bell hanging high above the roof. Her tug wasn't strong enough so she tugged again this time a little harder. The bell rang out a gentle sound so she tugged even harder. This time the bell was loud and clear. Children from all over the school yard slowly approached the stairway dragging their feet. The only one excited to begin their school year all over again was Sadie.

Once the children were all inside, Amelia began by introducing herself. "Good morning students. My name is Amelia Bradford-Cummings. I live here in Smithfield just down the road. I moved here several months ago so that I could find out some things that I didn't know. I have met most of you already and I want to get to know each and every one of you. Now, let's take care of the very first thing. Classe bonjour. Bonjour. The students gave Amelia a very funny look. None of them responded to her greeting. She repeated the words, classe, bonjour. Still there were looks of confusion on the student's faces. "Class, I just said good morning to you in French. We will be learning basic French and this is your first lesson. Good morning is said, bonjour. Now repeat it after me. Bonjour." There were many variations attempted of this simple word. Elliot Jr. said, "Why in the world do we need to learn a fancy new way of sayin' good mornin'? None of us will ever speak this fancy talk. We aren't goin' to France – ever. So why don't you just start talkin' like normal folk do here instead of makin' us say bonny jury. Sounds ridiculous to me." Ernest piped up, "Hush up Elliot. You never know when a little French speakin' would come in handy. Who knows, you just might end up in France someday and you're gonna wish you were payin' attention. You won't even know how to say good mornin'."

"I don't care how to say good mornin' in no French speak. It sounds stupid if you ask me."

Amelia just looked at Elliot and felt a moment of defeat. She gave Ernest a look of appreciation for defending her desire to teach the children something outside of Smithfield.

"Next class, we will learn how to count to ten in French. Now let's begin. One sounds like oone with a u sound. Repeat it after me. Oone." The class repeated the word as instructed. "Tomorrow we will work on saying the words good morning, one, and two until we can say basic phrases and count in French. Now it's time to cover the classroom rules. First things first - get to class on time. Have your supplies ready. Have your homework finished. Be quiet. Do not talk unless you are instructed to talk. Ask to talk by raising your hand. No running. No yelling. No calling each other names. Treat others with respect. Do not deface school property. Does everyone understand?"

The students all looked at each other with looks of utter confusion. It was a morning whirlwind of speaking fancy languages and rules on top of rules. No one seemed excited or eager to begin this new adventure except for Sadie who had a look on her face like she had done seen angels standing there teaching the students how to speak French.

Miss Amelia knew how to interpret the student's facial expressions and her assertion was absolutely correct – they were not fond of speaking French or hearing more rules. She changed her lesson plan just ever so slightly to accommodate the disinterested learners. She told the students to get out their slates and chalk. "Now students, let's play a game. I want you to write one word about yourself that perhaps no one else knows or something that everyone knows except for me. Take a few minutes to think about your answer and then write it on your slates. Don't show anyone your word. As a matter of fact, you can turn your slate over to hide your word."

The students sat quietly for a minute and then some started to write their word on their slates. Some took an extra long time to think of their word while others had theirs written pretty quickly.

"Time is up", said Amelia. "Do not turn over your slate until after I try to guess your word. Now, who wants to go first? Raise your hand."

None of the students raised their hand. Amelia volunteered Virginia to be first. "Virginia, I think you wrote the word friendly." Some of the student's snickered at Amelia's guess. Virginia turned her slate over and replied, "No Miss Amelia, I'm perfect." There was more laughter from the students this time. Amelia tried once again, "Sadie, let me guess your word." Elliot Jr. piped up in a very snide way. "Oh, that's real hard. You know Sadie very well."

Amelia tried to ignore Elliot's comment. "Sadie, you are compassionate." She turned over her slate and replied, "No, Miss Amelia. I wrote adventure. I like adventures. You should know that."

Amelia replied, "Yes, Sadie. I do know that you like to go on adventures; however, I also know that you are very compassionate. Elliot, you're next. I think you wrote protector. Elliot replied, "No, you're wrong. I wrote that I hate school and I hate this stupid game. What kind of word is protector? That doesn't describe me at all. Some teacher you are."

Sadie had all she could stand of her brother's angry attitude. "Stop it Elliot. You're bein' mean to Miss Amelia. She's just tryin' to get to know us better and you're not helpin'. Just you wait till we get home. I am tellin' on you real good. I'm tellin' dad cause he's on Miss Amelia's side."

"Shut up Sadie", Elliot replied. "I'm tellin' mom cause she's not on Miss Amelia's side."

Amelia became so upset that she ran out of the classroom to get a breath of fresh air. She started to cry but she knew that crying would only reinforce what others had already thought of her. After deep breathing for a couple of minutes, Amelia went back inside and gave the students an assignment.

"I'm sorry class for that interruption. Erase your slates and write these math problems up here on the board. No talking and no cheating off someone else's slate. Do these math problems until recess.

Time seemed to drag very slowly for the students and Amelia. It seemed like forever before the students could go outside for recess. The rest of the day seemed just as slow because the morning made for a very awkward uncomfortable day. Most all of the students were glad that the end of the school day was near but most of all Amelia. She didn't do much teaching that day, mostly she had students do work on the board or on their slates. The clock finally made its way to 3:00 and it was time to end this horrible experience. The students gathered their belongings and quickly ran out the door to go home. Once the last student left, Amelia

sat back down at her desk and started to cry.

59

8

I AM NOT GOING BACK – I QUIT

After Amelia cried for awhile, she gathered her things and walked home. She opened her front door and was greeted by Frederick. "Good afternoon Miss Amelia. How was your first day as Smithfield's new teacher?"

She looked at Frederick and he could tell that she had been crying. "It was horrible Frederick. I am not going back. I quit. I am not a teacher. Those kids hate me. These towns-people were right. I am not fit to be the teacher."

Frederick stood there quietly while he thought about what to say next. He really wasn't sure what to say that would make Amelia feel better. He offered to make her a cup of tea, but she didn't want any.

Amelia went to her room and shut the door behind her. She wasn't in any kind of mood to be social right now. She started to cry again with this feeling of complete failure. Soon after her time of crying, she drifted off to sleep. Frederick knew that she needed this time to be alone so he put supper on hold until she felt like eating. While he was waiting for Amelia to wake up, he thought about what to say to help her situation. He would say little, but he would do something.

Amelia finally woke from her nap feeling exhausted and emotionally drained. She wanted a glass of water and nothing else. Frederick offered to get the water for her as he saw this as his opportunity to help. Besides the glass of water, he handed her a small book. He said, "Read this please." She looked at him with much disinterest. Reading a book was the last thing that Amelia wanted to do. Amelia went back to her room with her water glass and this very plain looking book with no title or no author written on the front.

She carefully opened the book and what she saw caught her attention. The words written on the pages were not typed, but they were handwritten.

My dearest family. I am writing to you because I know that at some point and time in your life, you will encounter some very difficult circumstances that will challenge you to the very core. Everything that you have been taught and every value that you hold dear will at this time become questionable. Oh, not that you will abandon these things, but you will wonder why you have been raised to be a good person who was chosen to go through a very difficult time. I won't always be here to share my words of wisdom, so here they are to share for generations to come. Whenever you have made it through your difficult journey, write on the blank pages how you overcame your circumstance. Not only will you have my words of encouragement, you will have words from family members who made their way too. Pass the book to someone else who needs a little encouragement, but never forget the words from the people who contributed to these pages. Here is one story from me. I was a very young girl - perhaps 5 or 6 years old. Our family lived in southern England at the time. We did not have much in the way of fancier things. Our means were very humble indeed, but nonetheless, we were proud of what we did have. My father Herbert went out every day to find food to feed 8 people. I had 5 siblings all under ten years old. I happened to be the oldest at eleven. Some of the things we go through seem senseless and we often wonder why they happen, but they do. We can either

*succumb to the circumstance, or we can overcome and this is what I did,
but it was not easy. Father went out one day as usual to find us some
food. It had been a particularly hard winter and everything was frozen
solid – the ground, the water, and seemingly the air. Father was walking
near the woods by the pond. He saw a creature run to a spot of bushes
by the water. The creature was not very big, but perhaps enough to
make a nice hearty stew. It became stuck in the bushes so father went
over to catch it. Since the ground was so frozen, he lost his footing by
the bushes and fell onto the frozen water. He had a hold of the creature,
but when he tried to stand up, the creature slipped out of his hands and it
ran away. Father tried still to stand back up, but his shoes were slick on
the bottom. This frozen area of the pond he was laying on must have
been thinner than the rest because he heard a loud crack and down into
the frozen water he went. He was in the water a long time before
someone came to his rescue. He was way too frozen to recover. We
tried to warm him up, but he was just too far gone. He passed in my
arms as I was trying to warm his cold frozen body. This drove mother
mad. She was never the same after that. She left us kids alone to fend
for ourselves. Me being the oldest, I was responsible for raising the
younger kids. I could not be the mother and father that they just lost. I
had to do something that for me was unthinkable – I sent them to live*

with relatives. Margaret and Thomas went to live with an aunt and uncle. Henry went to live with a family from the neighboring farm. Caroline went to London to live with mother's cousin. Peter went to live in the orphanage, but I visited him often. I was taken by the constable to live with an affluent family. Well, it wasn't the royal family exactly, but I was raised by one of the family's nursemaids. I lived a life of privilege and wanted for nothing. I wanted so much to be reunited with my siblings, but that never happened. I could have become bitter and angry that in one afternoon my world changed forever, but I took that circumstance and learned how to overcome. I often felt like I never belonged to anyone, but I knew that I would never be alone. Adversity often makes us stronger if we allow ourselves to learn from it. Be strong. Be courageous. Hold up your head high. Don't be overcome by adversity. Draw from the strength you think you don't have. My best I leave with you now and forever. Madeline

Amelia sat there on her bed very still, she barely made any movement. She read the words from Madeline and was reminded of what she needed to do next. Amelia read the stories from other family members who faced adversity with their words of encouragement. Amelia went into the kitchen where Frederick was preparing the evening meal. She said, "Frederick, these stories are wonderful. What a beautiful legacy these family members have left behind. May I ask, who is the original author Madeline?" Frederick stood there a few minutes before answering. "Madeline is my mother. Herbert was my grandfather." Amelia replied, "Oh Frederick, I am amazed at these stories and I thank you for sharing them with me. I know now that this little ordeal with the children at school is very small in comparison to the things that your family has endured. No, I cannot quit, but I have to persevere and stay strong. These children deserve that. They deserve a teacher who can take the good and the bad. I think I can do this even though the road will be rough. The journey wouldn't be an adventure if the roads weren't a little bumpy along the way. Thank you Frederick."

Amelia gave Frederick a hug. She knew that from this point forward, she had to continue teaching. She asked Frederick if he would ever write something in the book. He replied, "Perhaps I might someday when the time is right." Frederick finished fixing supper as Amelia began to write notes on her stationery. She wrote, A New Beginning.

9

A NEW BEGINNING

Amelia and Frederick finished their supper. After all the dishes were done and the kitchen cleaned up, Amelia wrote some more notes on her stationery paper. She folded the gentle papers and then tucked them into her purse after she had written the last word. She felt more determined than ever to continue teaching. The stories from Frederick's book were very inspiring to continue through adversity.

The next day at school, some of the students came in with the same cynical looks as they did the day before. Instead of being shy and holding back, Amelia stood in front of the class with authority and determination. With a very firm voice she said, "Good morning class.

Today is a new day in more ways than just the obvious. Yes, we will continue to count and learn new words in French, but I think we should start this day with something a little more important. Get out your slates." A few of the students let out an audible moan. Amelia responded, "If moaning is on your list of things to do at school today, I suggest that you leave now. Today……this day is not the day to moan and complain. I have something very eye opening for you to do and I know that some of you will actually understand the value of this exercise. I am the teacher here because the mayor has faith in my abilities, but more important than that, I have faith in myself. You may not like me, but that's ok. It's your opinion not to like me or the things I chose to teach you; however, I am going to earn your respect. It is your choice to go home and tell your parents that I am an inadequate teacher not fit to teach; however, be careful with the measuring stick you use to judge others because the standard by which you measure others will come back upon you. It is my hopes that you will understand one day that the things I am trying to teach you. Now, on your slates, I want you to write one thing that has happened in your life that has made you sad or hurt your feelings. Do not share what you write with anyone else and do not look at someone else's slate. What you write is very personal and not to be shared with others for now. Someday you might want to share what you wrote, but right now it's yours to keep."

Elliot Jr piped up, "This is a dumb lesson. I don't have to do it. I see no point in writing this down. It has nothin' to do with learnin' anything. I won't write nothin' and you can't make me."

Amelia walked over to Elliot's desk and looked down at him with a very stern determined look. She said, "You have a choice Elliot Fuller. You can choose to sit here and defy everything I'm trying to do, or you can actually open up your mind to learn something. If you choose to learn, then by all means sit here and learn. If your choice is to refuse anything I'm trying to teach, then either go home or keep your mouth and your opinion closed while in my classroom. If you have something meaningful to say that will help the class understand the lesson better, then at least have the common decency to raise your hand and be acknowledged. If you are determined to cause a disturbance in my classroom and cause the other students to join in your shenanigans, then we will see to it that you won't have a problem with what I'm teaching because you won't be attending school here. Elliot Fuller, do you understand everything I just said to you?"

Elliot just sat there and said nothing for a minute. He then quietly responded to Amelia's question. "Yes ma'am. I understand. I might not like it, but I understand."

Amelia walked away from Elliot and continued, "Good. Since Elliot provided you with an extra couple of minutes to think and write, I am going to talk about the things that you have written, in general terms of course. I am looking at some of the things that you have written and no one can ever say that your feelings are not genuine. If someone hurt you, they hurt you. If someone offended you, they offended you. If someone said mean things to you, they said mean things. Don't ever let someone else determine your feelings. They are yours to have and yours to either let go or hold on to. You know the old saying about sticks and stones breaking your bones, but the words other people say to us do not hurt? Well, it isn't true. Words are very powerful things. They have the power to build up, to tear down, to destroy, to hurt, to offend, to praise, to challenge, to chastise, and to encourage. I am not going to lie to you, but yesterday my feelings were hurt by your actions and words. It was my intent to tell the mayor today and I quit. I never wanted to come back here and face another day like yesterday. However, I chose to let your words go and not influence what I know and believe. I know I am a capable person who can teach you things you've never even thought of before. I can help bring the world to you and hope to inspire a love for learning. I can do that if you let me. Some of you will never leave

Smithfield, and that is ok. But, some of you will venture off to other parts of the world. You will see amazing things that will be forever etched in your memories. You will also see some things that will make you wonder why these things are happening to other people. Regardless of where your path takes you, people have feelings and the things that you say and do to others will either building them up, challenge them, or tear them down. That choice is yours. Then, that person has the choice to allow one of those things to happen. Based on your words and actions yesterday, I choose challenge. You have made me more determined than ever to be the best teacher this town has ever had. Those are my true feelings class. You have inspired me to be better.

Now, I want you to think about what you wrote on your slates. Think about the feelings that you had or still have when someone hurt you or about the time when you were sad. Now, make a decision. Decide what you are going to do with these feelings. Are you going to keep these feelings or let them go? That's your choice. Are you going to let these feelings build you up, challenge you, or tear you down? Think carefully before you decide."

10

IT FINALLY CLICKED

Amelia's discussion with the students about genuine feelings was the turning point for the students of Smithfield. From that day on, the students came in ready to learn. They were excited to learn new French words and discover new ideas. Each day was a fresh new opportunity for the students to explore the world around them. Even Elliot Jr. eventually came around and enjoyed going to school. He never really came out and said that he did, but he didn't give Miss Amelia a hard time from that day forward.

One day after school,   Sadie started walking toward her daddy's auto repair shop. She was going to stop by there to get a ride home in the old truck. Sadie looked behind her and she saw Ernest following in the distance. He turned his head quickly when Sadie saw him. He pretended that he didn't notice her, but he did indeed notice her. He had been watching her the whole time. Sadie stopped walking, turned around and asked Ernest, "Why are you following me. Don't deny it cause I've been hearin' your footsteps behind me. You can't pull wool over my eyes Ernest."

"Can I walk you home Sadie?"

"No you can't walk me home cause I ain't goin' home. I'm going to my daddy's shop to get a ride home. So go on now. Walk on home."

"Can I at least talk to you Sadie?"

"Bout what?" Seems nothin' much to talk about. We just talked at school about the change in the weather comin' soon."

"That was the whole class talkin'. I wanna talk just to you."

"Oh, Ernest. You are still just as silly as ever. What could we possibly talk about?"

"Sadie, I....I....I....I really, really like you. I always have and I always will. I never had no courage to tell you before, so now I did. I told you. There. See, that wasn't so bad, now was it."

"Ernest, I'd have to be as blind as a bat to not see that you've liked me since forever. Look, if anyone at school found out that you liked me, I would get teased and tormented all day. No thank you. I'll have none of that teasin' going on. I am much obliged that you think of me that way, but I just can't accept it."

"Sadie, you know what I like about you?"

"Ernest, please just stop. Quit talkin'. The more talkin' you do, the more silly you sound. There are plenty of other girls at school you could take a likin' to. Tell one of them what you just said to me. I know Virginia would faint like a bird shot out of a tree if she heard you say these things to her. Why don't you just go on and like someone else?"

"Sadie, I like you cause you aren't like the other girls. They are ok, but you are somethin' special. You like frogs and fishin' and they don't. You like to play stick ball but all them girls wanna do is gossip and tell stories that ain't true. Sadie, you are the kind of gal that a guy like me can settle down with. You know, get hitched someday. You make my heart all flutter like a whole field full of butterflies. My belly gets all knotted up whenever you walk by me at school. Sadie, you are my gal and one day, one day I am gonna marry you. Yep, there I said it. I've been sayin' it every day to myself for years and I finally said it out loud."

"Ernest, you can't say things like that because they ain't......... they ain't."

"Ain't what Sadie?"

"Ain't.........supposed........to......be......said.......now. Come on now Ernest. Snap outta this here crazy thinkin' that's goin' on in your head. I don't wanna get married. I just might not be the marryin' kind you know. I don't wanna settle down here in Smithfield. I wanna explore the world and see those things that need to be seen. I wanna go to those places that we read about in those picture books. If there's a mountain to climb, I wanna climb it. If there's a river to cross, I wanna cross it. I wanna go on adventures to the grandest places ever imaginable. I can't do all these things with my feet firmly planted here in Smithfield. Settlin' down and having a bushel full of kids won't do nothin' but tie my feet down here and that's not what I wanna do. It's not how I wanna live my life. Livin' in Smithfield is fine for most folk, but it's not fine for me. I'm tellin' ya Ernest, one day I will pack my bags and head to who knows where. I'll be back of course, but not 'til I have experienced that grand adventure. Then, maybe after I've had my adventures and grow to a ripe old age of 30, I'll come back and think about getting' hitched. But until then, it's off on those grand adventures.

"

"I just had to tell you now Sadie before someone else comes along and sweeps up your feet. I would just die a thousand deaths if that happened. I would knowed for sure that Ernest is the grandest chickens of all time. Too chicken to tell Sadie how he's felt all these years and now cause he's the biggest chicken, someone else done carried her away. Everyone will say, look at Ernest, the big chicken. Now his precious Sadie Mae is hitched to someone else cause he was a chicken. I knowed how you do things Sadie Mae Fuller. You're gonna go off on one of them adventures and find yourself a man of sophistication. One who knows how to speak that French talk that Miss Amelia teaches us every day. He will go off on adventures with you too and you'll never think of us ever again. Sadie, my heart belongs to you and no one else. I think about you every moment of every day. There ain't one second of my day that doesn't have you in it even if it is only in my thoughts."

"Ernest, I have to tell you something too. Something I've needed to say to you for a very long time."

At that moment, they arrived at Elliot Sr.'s auto repair shop. Sadie stopped just in front of the shop door. She looked at Ernest and saw the look of despair on his forlorn face. At that moment she saw inside

Ernest's heart. She saw his sincere feelings of love and devotion. Sadie definitely didn't want her daddy to hear what she needed to say to Ernest. She told Ernest that she would see him tomorrow at school and that he should run on home. Ernest turned away with his hands in his pockets and his head hung low. Sadie would have to wait another day to tell Ernest her secret.

11

THE MERRIEST OF SEASONS

Just a few weeks after Miss Amelia accepted the teaching job, the

anticipation for Thanksgiving rested on each resident of Smithfield,

especially the students. Thanksgiving meant food and lots of it. At the

Fuller house, Elliot Sr. hunted the woods for just the right animal,

whether it be bird, pig, deer, or whatever else looked good that day.

Beverly would whip up a mighty fine dinner of vegetable stew,

cornbread, apple and pumpkin pie, and Sadie's favorite – chicken and

dumplings. Whenever Bev made chicken and dumplings, she had to

make a huge pot because all of the Fuller family liked her dumplings. It just might be safe to say that Bev's dumplings were the best in all of Fulton County.

One time when the church had a dinner on the ground, Bev brought a big pot of those dumplings, but so did Myrtle Smith. Elliot Jr. embarrassed Bev real good. While the reverend was reaching for a big heapin' spoonful of Myrtle's dumplings, Elliot Jr. said, "Hey reverend, them there dumplings ain't my momma's. Them dumplings are old Myrtle Smith's. They ain't as good as momma's. I'll eat no other dumplings cause they just ain't as good." Unfortunately, Myrtle heard Elliot's comments and she scolded him real good. The reverend had to come between the two of them to keep Myrtle from giving Elliot a piece of her mind. Bev quickly came over and apologized for Elliot's comments. He just kept saying that it was the truth and everyone done knowed it. From that day forward, Myrtle never brought her dumplings to a church dinner ever again.

Thanksgiving day finally arrived. As usual, Elliot Sr. loaded up his gun, put on his boots and warm jacket, and headed off to the woods. He told Elliot Jr. that one day he could go hunting with him. While Elliot Sr. was off hunting, Bev began a whole day of cooking. She started with boiling the chicken for the dumplings. Then she made the dough for the dumplings out of flour, water, and other ingredients. She never used a recipe. She just knew how much to add because her momma taught her how to make them dumplings and she's made them thousands of times. The next thing that Bev would do is to get the dough made for the pies. Her pie crusts were almost as famous as her dumplings. She could make pie crusts from memory too. All her recipes were up inside her head.

Bev never cooked alone. She always enlisted the help of one or more of the Fuller children. She put them to work peeling vegetables and fruits, mixing ingredients, and cleaning up as she was cooking. Normally, the Fuller children didn't like helping Bev in the kitchen, but Thanksgiving Day was much different. All of their favorite foods were cooked on this day. The house began to smell wonderful with the aroma of many different but very familiar smells. Sadie's favorite smells were the chickens boiling and the pumpkin pies baking. You could tell it was Thanksgiving just by the smells.

Elliot Sr. finally came home after a couple of hours out in the woods. He carried in two ducks that he had shot out of the sky. He actually shot four ducks, but he always hunts a little extra for those in need. He always helped Bev clean the animals that he brought in to be eaten. The oven fire was good and hot – ready for them ducks. When the ducks started cooking real good, the kitchen filled with another wonderful smell – roasted duck. Sadie never really noticed it before, but Bev would always make a little extra food and set it aside, but it never went to the table. She always made more pies than what their family could eat. Sadie never mentioned it before, but this year she was curious why Bev made extra food.

With all of the food properly prepared and the table set full of fine vittles, the Fuller family began each meal with a prayer. This prayer was the most special prayer of the year. Elliot Sr. said, "Everyone please bow your head as we give our thanks this day." Everyone bowed their head as requested. He continued, "Father in heaven above. We thank you for your many blessings on our family and on those in Smithfield. We ask that in these days of want and plenty that you continue to provide just what we need. Help those who are less fortunate. Send someone to help those who have little. Help us do our part to lend a hand. Watch over us and protect us. We give you thanks for all of your many blessing and may we never forget from where those blessings come. Amen." Everyone else repeated amen too.

As the Fuller family enjoyed their Thanksgiving meal, Sadie decided to ask about the extra food. She asked, "Momma, why do you always cook extra food, but it never gets put out on the table?"

Bev replied, "Sadie, God has blessed us with plenty of food. On each Thanksgiving Day, your daddy takes the extra food and gives it to a family that doesn't have as much. We don't wanna take away their pride, so he just sets it on their porch and walks away. We can bless others by giving our extra. It's the least we can do to show ourselves to be a good neighbor and community. We take care of others who have a hard time taking care of themselves, but we do it so they have their pride."

Sadie quickly replied, "That's what I did for them girls in St. Louis. They had no food and I gave them some. They had on what looked like nice dresses, but they were dirty and torn. They said their house got taken by the bank and they had to live outside without a home. Can I go with daddy this time? Oh, please! I wanna go take food to someone who doesn't have much. I won't whisper a word to anyone about it. Them St. Louis girls were scared about takin' food, but they were thankful to get it. Daddy, can I go with you?"

Elliot Sr. said, "Yes, Sadie. You can go, but you have to remember that this is our family secret and you keep that secret with you always. Just cause we give to someone else, doesn't mean we have to make it known to everyone else. That's not the spirit of true giving." Sadie and Elliot Sr. took the extra food, enough to feed two families, to those in need. Sadie kept her secret and never told anyone.

After Thanksgiving was over, the Fuller children knew that Christmas wouldn't be too far behind. A couple of weeks before Christmas, Elliot Sr. would again go to the woods, but this time for the tree. Bev would always give him instructions by which would produce the most perfect tree – one with even branches and short needles. As Elliot Sr. was in the forest hunting for the Christmas tree, Bev had the children make decorations to place on it.   The children took thin pieces of paper that they colored and drew pictures on and made a paste out of flour and water. They glued the thin pieces of paper into circles to make a long chain to put around the tree. After the paper chain was made, Bev would pop a huge pot of popcorn. She gave the oldest children a needle with a long string of thread. The children strung the pieces of popcorn on the thread and made a garland out of popcorn. Then the children made star-shaped ornaments out of a thick dough made of flour, water, and salt.

Christmas morning was the most enjoyable time for the Fuller children. They always hung their stockings Christmas Eve in anticipation of them being filled with goodies the next morning. Sadie always had a hard time falling asleep the night before Christmas because she knew that there would be something special for them in their stockings.

Elliot Sr. would always read the Christmas story out of the Bible from the second chapter of Luke. He always said, "This is the true meaning of Christmas." After he read the story, we were given our stockings, one by one. This year their stockings were filled with nuts from the walnut and pecan trees, an apple, one piece of sugar candy, mittens that Bev had knitted, and a scarf. All of the children were especially grateful for the things they received that day.

12

A BIRTHDAY SURPRISE

The months had passed and now spring was evident by the blooming flowers and warmer days. By the signs from nature, Sadie knew that her birthday would be coming up soon. Every year for her birthday, Bev made Sadie a new dress. Sadie always appreciated a new dress to wear.

On Thursday, April 20th after school, Sadie was walking home and stopped by a field that was covered in tall yellow weeds. She sat in the field enjoying the warm sun and the smell of green grass and flowers. Her eyes were closed as she sat with the warm sun beating down on her face. She was suddenly startled when someone quickly sat down beside her. It was Ernest.

"Why do you always try and scare me like that. I could have been scared to death you know."

"Oh, don't be a baby Sadie Fuller. Don't be so skiddish."

"I'm not skiddish Ernest. I just don't like someone sneaking up on me."

Ernest had been hiding something behind him, but he brought it in front of him and handed it to Sadie.

"What's these for Ernest. They're weeds?"

"Why these here are your birthday flowers. Don't you remember your birthday flowers. On your birthday a few years ago I gave you a handful of flowers. I think I was seven at the time and you were six. I told you months ago I've always loved you even when we were kids. So here, take them." Sadie took the yellow weeds and smelled them.

"I need to go Ernest. Miss Amelia wants me to come by her house today. I'm not sure why, but I gotta go."

"Aw, Sadie. Just stay one more minute, please."

"No Ernest. I promised her I would come by before I went home. I will see you tomorrow at school. And thank you for the wee……flowers." Sadie reached over and gave Ernest a kiss on the cheek. He sat there frozen and amazed. Sadie quickly got up and ran toward Amelia's house.

Sadie knocked on Amelia's front door and as always, Frederick opened the door with a greeting. "Hello Miss. May I ask who comes calling on this very fine and special day?"

"Oh, you silly Frederick. You know it's me Sadie. Miss Amelia wanted to see me today."

"Why yes. I will let her know you are here. Please, come and sit down and wait for her here."

Frederick left the room and left Sadie alone in the sitting room. A few minutes later he returned announcing the presence of Amelia.

"Good day Sadie. How do you do?"

"Miss Amelia, you should know how I do. I just saw you at school."

Amelia cleared her throat. "Well, this I know to be a very special day because it is your birthday. Happy birthday Sadie. May this be one of many special happy birthdays. I have a present for you." Amelia handed Sadie a package wrapped in beautiful paper and tied in a big pink bow. Sadie held the package in her hand and didn't want to open it because it was so beautiful. She slowly pulled back the perfectly folded paper held down flat with tape. Sadie gently pulled back the paper to reveal a plain brown box. She looked at the box carefully and started to open it. Inside the box was thin white paper and something underneath. She moved the thin white paper to reveal something amazing inside. It was Miss Amelia's snow globe from her honeymoon in Paris. Sadie's eyes grew wide as the gazed upon the trinket that caught her eye about a year ago.

"Oh Miss Amelia! I can't take your snow globe. This is something real special from Albert on your honeymoon. I just can't accept it. I love it, but it's yours."

"Sadie Mae Fuller, it is mine to give to whom I see fit. I want you to have it because I know you will keep it safe and cherish your precious tower. One day you will see this tower for yourself and I hope you will think fondly of me. I want this globe to bring happy memories instead of sad ones. Now, it's time to think about happy things and good times to come. Enjoy it Sadie. It's yours."

Sadie just sat there overwhelmed at her gift. Suddenly there was a knock on the door. Frederick and Amelia looked puzzled because they were not expecting any other visitors. Frederick opened the door and was handed a telegram addressed to Miss Amelia. He took the telegram to Amelia who opened it up carefully.

It read:

To Amelia Bradford-Cummings – Stop – Your Aunt Jacqueline has been admitted to the hospital – Stop – She is in serious condition – Stop – We do not expect her to pull through – Stop – She is asking to see you – Stop – Dr. Frank Malloy

89